THE OLDEN DAYS COAT

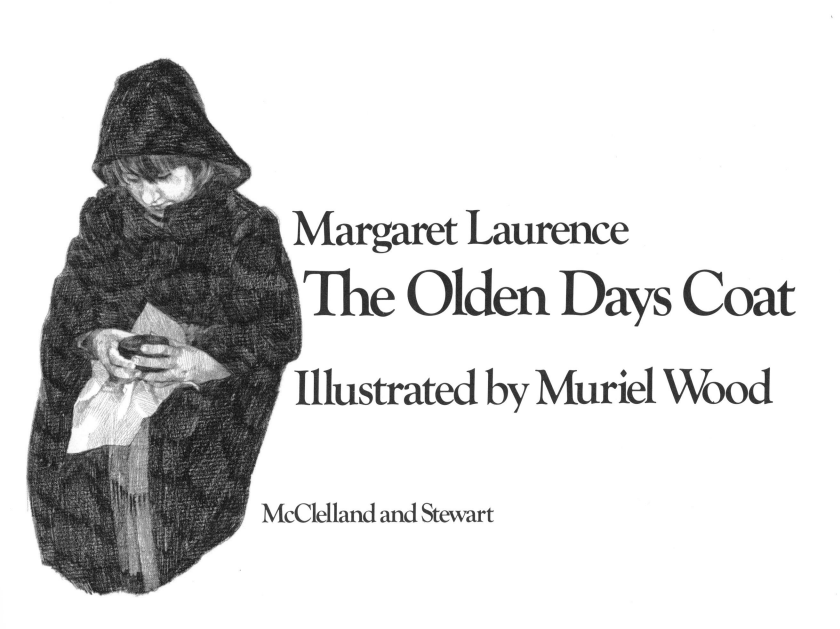

Margaret Laurence
The Olden Days Coat

Illustrated by Muriel Wood

McClelland and Stewart

for my friend
Tamara Stone
who was ten when this book
was first published

Text: Copyright © 1979 Margaret Laurence
Illustration: Copyright © 1979 and 1982 Muriel Wood

Hardcover edition 1982
Reprinted 1983
ISBN: 0-7710-4742-8

The Canadian Publishers
McClelland and Stewart Limited
25 Hollinger Road
Toronto, Ontario M4B 3G2

CANADIAN CATALOGUING IN PUBLICATION DATA

Laurence, Margaret, 1926-
   The olden days coat

ISBN: 0-7710-4742-8

I. Wood, Muriel.   II. Title.

PS8523.A86043   jC813′.5′4   C79-094464-2
PZ7.L390l

Printed and bound in Canada

The snow outside Gran's house was fine and powdery, and it shone in the late afternoon sun as though there were a million miniature Christmas lights within it. The bare branches of the maples cast blue shadows across the white expanse of the lawn. Sal thought briefly of lying down in the fresh snow and sweeping her arms to and fro to make a snow angel, but the snow looked so good as it was, with not even a footprint in it, she decided to leave it that way.

The village street was quiet; no one in sight, and the old yellow or red brick houses were solid and serene, their front porches decorated with spruce-bough wreaths and coloured lights. Sal felt she ought to be happy, but she was not. She was depressed, miserable, and sad, and at the same time slightly ashamed of herself for feeling this way.

It wasn't that Sal didn't like visiting her grandmother. Any other week of the entire year would have been just great. But tomorrow would be the first Christmas Day of all the ten Christmases of Sal's life that she wouldn't be spending in her own home. Even though

Mother and Dad were here, and even though Gran was a terrific person, it wasn't the same. As long as Sal could remember, Gran and Grandad had spent Christmas in the city with Sal and her parents. But Grandad had died this year, and Sal still missed him and could hardly believe she wouldn't see him again. Gran hadn't been too well lately.

"She'd like to spend Christmas at her place, Sal," Mother had said. "I think she'd like – oh, I don't know – I just have the feeling that she'd like to have at least this one Christmas in her own home right now."

It had been a new thought to Sal that Gran might want Christmas in her own home, just as Sal wanted Christmas in *her* own home.

"But she and Grandad always spent Christmas at our house!" Sal had almost shouted. "Didn't she *want* to, all those times?"

"Sure, she wanted to," Mother had replied gently. "But now, with Grandad having died – well, she misses him a lot, Sal. And their house in the village is the one they lived in together for so many years."

If Sal missed Grandad a lot, how must Gran feel? All at once Sal had seen how her grandmother must feel. So naturally she had to agree and try to act pleased at the idea of the trip, even though she wouldn't be seeing Marian or Kathie or any of the other kids on Christmas afternoon to compare presents, and wouldn't be going to the Christmas Eve carol service with them all, and wouldn't see her own special decorations on the tree – the tiny golden and blue glass peacock, the silver bells, the little Santa Claus, and all the others that had been a part of Christmas, it seemed, forever. Sal didn't want things to change. Of course, things *did* change, and you had to get used to it, but sometimes it wasn't all that easy.

So here she was at Gran's place, not knowing even one kid her own age in the village, and *bored.* What was there to do? Answer: Nothing. Mother and Dad and Gran were all in the house, tearing around doing things – last-minute present-wrapping, making the

stuffing for the turkey, and so on and so on. They had asked her to help, but Sal just didn't feel like it. She had said she was going outside for awhile to play. Play! Play what, and who with?

Then Sal remembered the shed behind Gran's house, and what was kept there. The door was a bit difficult to open, but Sal finally creaked the hinges into action. Good – the old trunk was still there, and inside it the photograph albums. On nearly every visit, Sal's dad would say, *Mother, shouldn't all that stuff be in the house?* And Gran would say, very polite but firm, *The shed's dry and I've got no room for another blessed thing in this house, James, and anyway, the past is in my mind – I've got no great need for photographs.* Sal wondered what it would be like to have all that long past in your mind.

She leafed through the albums. Some of the pictures were a pale brown colour, faded, and some were shadowy black and white. None were in colour, for they'd been taken before the days of colour film. How peculiar they looked. Pictures of the village when it was even smaller than it was today, pictures of people sitting in high-up little carts pulled by horses, pictures of families all dressed up and sitting on front porches, pictures of square-shaped tinny-looking olden days cars. A picture of Gran as a young woman, her hair braided and fixed very nicely across the top of her head, her long dress patterned with small flowers. Another of Gran, some years later but still young-looking, with her hair cut shorter and dress also much shorter, standing on the steps of the brick house, which was then new. How long ago it must have been.

Imagine that young woman there being *Gran.* It almost seemed as though it must be a photograph of somebody else entirely. But Gran's name was printed under the picture, and there was Gran's

same smile and the same eyes looking friendly and – well, *interested*. What a strange thing Time was. It went on and on, and people came into it and then went out again, like Grandad. There was a time when she, Sal, had not even existed, and now here she was, and would grow up and maybe have children of her own. Maybe someday she would even have a grand-daughter. It was as hard for Sal to think of herself being old like Gran as it was to think of Gran having once been ten years old.

Sal picked up another album, and the pages fell open at a photograph of a girl about her own age, a really old-fashioned girl with a floppy bow in her long hair, and wearing a frilly dress down past her knees with a huge wide sash at the waist, and – look at that! – striped stockings and high buttoned boots! Why on earth did people wear such funny clothes away back then?

Sal chortled to herself, then suddenly stopped. Years and years from now, would her own jeans and T-shirt, or even her dress-up long skirts, look funny to some other kid? Maybe even to her own grand-daughter? What a weird thought. And could this photo right here be Gran as a kid? It didn't say, and it was impossible to tell. This girl was sort of frowning and you couldn't see her eyes clearly at all. She looked uncomfortable, as though she wasn't enjoying having her picture taken, all dressed up like that. No wonder. The frilly dress had dozens of little buttons down the front – imagine doing all those up! – and the sash looked too tight.

Sal put down the album and dug deeper into the trunk. She came up with something she had never noticed before on other visits to Gran's place. A girl's coat. An olden days coat. It was dark navy blue, with a hood, and at the waist there was attached a narrow red wool sash. It looked as though it might fit Sal. She decided to try it on. She slipped out of her own coat and into the old one. It fitted her perfectly.

And then –

Sal felt all at once very dizzy. There was a moment of darkness, and she wondered if she was fainting. She had never fainted, so she did not know how it might feel. She decided it wouldn't feel like this. For an instant or for a long time (she wasn't sure which), Sal didn't think anything. It was not like sleep. Rather, it was like going away from yourself for awhile. Like losing track of time. And yet, oddly enough, she wasn't afraid.

* * * *

Sal rubbed her eyes and looked around her. She was standing outside in the snow. How had that happened? She did not recall having

left the shed. It must have snowed a whole lot more since she entered the shed. How long had she been in there, anyway? The snow was now nearly up to the top of her boots. She was wearing the navy blue coat with the hood, and the scarlet sash was tied around her middle. But she didn't have her gloves. She had taken them off to look at the photograph albums. She turned back to the shed to get them. And then she gazed around in total bewilderment.

The shed was not there.

Sal swung around to face Gran's house. Now she knew for sure that something very odd was happening. The house was not there, either.

Where was she?

Across the road, the old church still stood. Thank goodness for that. At least she was still in the village. But wait – some of the other houses on the street were missing, too. And neither the street lights nor the telephone poles were anywhere to be seen. There were no TV aerials. The maple trees were there, but they looked different. They were much smaller. Trees could grow (although not quickly) but surely they couldn't shrink?

For a moment, Sal felt a sense of panic. *Where am I? Where am I?* Then she remembered the photograph albums. The street looked very much like some of the earliest photographs. Could it be that she was in some different time? How could that be? Yet here she was. *Wait a minute,* she said to herself. *Hold on, here. Let's think, now.* She had put on the olden days coat. And then the feeling of losing track of time. Those things must be connected. But if she really was in some other time, how to get back – or, as it would be, forward? She had thought this was going to be a boring Christmas, and now look what had happened. Would she ever return to her own family? And if she didn't, then what? That was a possibility too terrible to think about, at least for now. As long as she was here (wherever *here* was), she might as well have a good look around.

Sal began walking, and in no time she was out of the village and into the open country. The narrow path enabled her to walk without much difficulty. It had not been ploughed by a snow-plough,

that was plain enough. But the snow was hard-packed and there were marks on it made by – what? Not cars. Not trucks. Not wheels of any kind, it seemed. What had made that double set of smooth tracks in the snow?

The boughs of the spruce and cedar trees glistened with snow and icicles as though they were newly decorated Christmas trees. Sal put her hands into the coat pockets and trudged along, now feeling almost light-hearted and confident. She felt in her bones that something was going to happen, something interesting, and she was eager to know what it would be.

When it did happen, however, Sal was so startled she nearly fell into a snowdrift. The sound of horses' hooves. The sound of bells.

"Whoa, Brownie! Whoa, Star!"

It was a girl's voice, loud and strong. Before Sal knew what was happening, the sleigh drew up beside her. Of course – the tracks in the snow had been made by big sleighs. Not the little sleighs that Sal had always known, that you pulled by yourself to the top of a slope, if you could find one in the park, and then got on and whizzed down. This sleigh was no toy. It had seats for two people at the front and two at the back. It was built gracefully, like a big swan-shaped boat, and it was painted a bright crimson with gold swirls. Underneath it were long sleigh-runners of metal and wood, curving up at the front. Pulling it were two sleek brown horses with bells on their harness. The driver was a girl who looked about Sal's age and size. She had warm brown eyes, mischievous and friendly, a slightly upturned nose, and a wide grin. She was dressed in a tight-fitting black coat, and she had blue wool mitts on her hands and a blue wool knitted bonnet on her head. Around her knees was tucked a sort of blanket of coarse straggly fur.

"Hello there!" she called out to Sal. "Where are you bound for? Do you want a ride?"

A ride in that sleigh? Sal certainly did. She climbed in, and the girl motioned to her to tuck the fur robe around her legs. Then, all at once, Sal felt not only shy but nervous. This strange girl was going to ask questions, and Sal was not at all sure how she could answer them.

"I haven't seen you in these parts before," the girl said. "Who would you be, then?"

Think quickly, Sal said to herself. *And it better not be a lie, either,* she told herself sternly. But how to tell the truth about the situation

when she wasn't even sure what the truth was? She somehow knew deep inside her that if she was ever going to get home again she must not tell any lies. This was going to be tricky.

"Oh – we don't belong in the village," Sal said hesitantly. "We are just spending Christmas here with a relative."

The girl's next question almost certainly would be *Who's your relative?* Everybody would know everybody else here. It was a small place. And then Sal really would be in trouble. She glanced around her, searching for a way to change the subject. Her eyes caught a flash of blue and white.

"Look!" she cried. "That bird! What is it?"

"It's a bluejay," the girl said. "Cheeky little things, those jays. I tame them in the winter, and they'll take bread from my hand. Sometimes I throw bits of fat or bacon rinds into the snow for them, and they always find them. They often follow me, just in the hopes of some food."

"Really?" Sal said, impressed. A girl who could tame birds and drive a team of horses – Sal had never known anybody who could do those things. But of course there weren't many horses around nowadays. *Nowadays?* Sal felt confused all over again about where she was, and when.

"My name's Sal," she said, as though to make quite sure of at least one thing. "What's yours?"

"Sarah," the strange girl said. "We live at New Grange Farm."

"Are you allowed – I mean, do you often take out the sleigh and horses by yourself?"

Sarah laughed. "I can take the cutter out almost any time I like. Papa knows I'm as good as my brothers with the horses."

Sal felt a twinge of envy. Imagine being able to go out in this sleigh (*cutter* – she must remember its name) any time you wanted. She wondered if Sarah felt lucky or if she took it for granted because it was what lots of people did, here.

The horses plunged onward, their harness bells jangling. The cutter sped through stands of spruce and pine, glittering and shimmering with the snow on their boughs. Sal thought it was the most exciting ride she'd ever had in her entire life, even counting the Giant Ferris Wheel at the Exhibition.

"I've been over to my best friend's house," Sarah was saying. "I wanted to show her my Early Present. We're always allowed to open one before Christmas Day."

"Oh, do you do that?" Sal cried. "We always have an Early Present, too."

This detail made her feel quite close to Sarah, and she sensed that Sarah felt the same.

"What was your Early Present, Sarah?" Sal asked curiously.

Sarah dug in her coat pocket, holding the horses' reins easily with one hand, and brought out a small object wrapped in red tissue paper. She handed it to Sal.

"Here – look. Papa carved it for me, and Mama did the painting. I shall cherish it always. I'll hand it on, I really will, to my children and their children. Papa and Mama laughed when I said that, but I think they were a bit pleased, too."

Sal unfolded the paper carefully. Inside was a carved wooden box. On the top, its wings delicately shaped in wood and painted a glowing orange and black, was a Monarch butterfly. Sal knew it was a Monarch, because her dad had pointed out that kind of butterfly to her on a visit to the village last spring. They were called Monarchs, Dad had said, because they were like the kings and queens of all the butterflies. On the underside of the box were these words – *To Sarah, from her loving parents.*

"It's beautiful," Sal said. "I've never seen anything like it."

"Won't you come and meet my family, Sal?" Sarah asked. "They'd be glad to meet you, I know, and your folks wouldn't worry for a little while, would they? I could take you back to the village later on."

Sal gulped. *Danger.* Meeting Sarah had been like getting a special and unexpected Christmas present. But going to New Grange Farm – that was something different. She just could not do it. But how could she get out of doing it?

If Sal went to the farm, as soon as she undid the olden days coat Sarah and her family would see that Sal's clothes were not at all the kind worn here in this place. They wouldn't understand, and how could she ever explain? You couldn't go into a welcoming house and not take off your coat, that was for sure. But she could not take the coat off *there*. She mustn't. It was her only chance of getting back home, and if she tried it at the wrong moment and in the wrong place –

Sal was all at once terrified.

She might never be able to return to her own place, her own family. Sal felt tears wanting to come into her eyes. She blinked them back furiously. This was no time for feeling sorry for herself. Action was what was needed, and that action had to be her own. Sarah was totally unaware of the danger, and she must remain so. It was up to Sal to find a solution.

What was she to say to Sarah? How could she, without being unkind and ungrateful, get out of the sleigh? She certainly could use a little help, Sal thought.

Sal had just handed the carved wooden box back to Sarah, and was frantically searching for an answer to Sarah's invitation, when a shower of huge icicles, sharp swords of frozen water, snapped and fell from a tree bough, directly in front of the horses.

CRASH!

The horses reared in fright, and bolted away down the snow path. The carved box flew out of Sarah's hands as she grabbed for the

reins that had been torn from her grasp. She snatched the reins back again, and pulled hard. But the box was gone.

"My box!" Sarah shouted. She soothed the horses then, her voice coaxing them out of their fear, and finally she brought the cutter to a halt.

"I'm going to go and look for it," Sal offered quickly. "You hold the horses, eh?"

Sarah agreed, and Sal ran back along the path through the forest. To find the box seemed an impossible task in all that snow. Supposing it had fallen into one of the deep drifts? No one would ever be able to find it. Sal located the place where the horses had reared, and began looking.

Hopeless.

Then she noticed a bluejay, hovering a few inches above the snow, darting down, searching for something. The bird settled and began to explore the snow.

Sal rushed over and shooed the bird away. *Sorry, bird,* she whispered under her breath, *better luck to you next time, but thanks.* She scooped away the soft light snow with her hands. And there it was. Nestling in the snow, quite unharmed, was the precious box. Sal snatched it up and ran back to Sarah.

"The jay found it, Sarah! The jay found it! He thought it was food, and he found it. Here it is!"

Sarah took the box and grinned.

"Oh Sal, how can I ever thank you? Now you'll surely come home with me."

Sal remained standing on the path. This was her only chance, and she knew it. Now if she could just do it right.

"Sarah, I'd love to, I really would. But I can't. My family will be worried. No – I know what you're going to say – you don't have to drive me back, but thanks anyway. It's not that far, and not that cold. I have to go. But I'll always be glad I met you."

No lies there. Not a one. Now if only the rest of it would work out.

Sarah nodded in understanding. The horses wanted to be going on again, so she drew gently in a little on the reins, reassuring them that they'd soon be off and away.

"Maybe we'll see each other, over the Christmas, then," Sarah said.

"Maybe," Sal said doubtfully. She wished with all her heart that such a meeting could be.

The two girls said a warm goodbye, and Sarah turned to flick the reins and tell the horses to go on.

Now was the moment for Sal's desperate plan. The timing had to be absolutely right, or she was done for. It had certainly been the putting-on of the olden days coat that had brought her here. It must be the taking-off of the coat that would take her home again. But the coat had to be tossed into the back of the cutter for the plan to work. Would she be able to do it swiftly enough, before the sleigh sped away? And would she be able to do it so that Sarah would not notice? She had to risk it.

Sal had already untied the red wool sash of the coat. As the cutter started up again, she slithered speedily out of the coat. In a flash, she had flung it into the back seat of the sleigh. It landed with a plop. The sleigh bells were ringing out. The horses were dashing along.

Sarah, guiding the horses, didn't notice the thrown coat and didn't look back at Sal shivering without a coat in the snow.

Sal had a split second to realize that the coat would go to New Grange Farm, and that there would be some good reason, unknown to her, for its being there. It would travel through history until –

BLACKNESS. Sal lost track of time. Everything blurred and faded.

* * * *

Sal opened her eyes.

She was sitting on the shed floor with her coat beside her. How

come? And yet she didn't feel cold. She put on her coat and looked around her. The photograph albums of long ago were spread out on the floor. She picked them up and began putting them back in the trunk. As she did so, she noticed something.

There, on the bottom of the trunk, neatly folded, was an olden days coat, a girl's coat. It was a dark navy blue, with a hood, and at the waist there was attached a narrow red wool sash. It looked as though it might fit Sal, and for a moment she thought of trying it on. But just then a voice boomed into the shed.

"Hey! So this is where you've been all this time. Did you go to sleep, or what? Lucky it's fairly warm out for this time of year. We've been a little worried about you."

Dad was standing in the shed doorway, grinning.

"I – I don't know," Sal said. "I was looking at the old albums, and I guess I sort of lost track of time. What time is it now, anyway?"

"Just time to open your Early Present," Dad said.

Gran and Mother were sitting in the living room. Sal had to admit that the tree that they'd decorated since she'd been out was really splendid, even though the ornaments were not those she was used to. Then she saw the peacock and the silver bells and the small Santa, there on the tree. Her own ornaments were there.

"You brought them!" she cried.

"We thought you'd like to see them on the tree as usual," Mother said, hugging Sal.

Gran was tall and thin, and her hands were gnarled like old tree branches. She was wearing her favourite brown and blue silk dress and the gold necklace that Grandad had given her long ago. Her hair was a feathery white. She didn't look a bit old-fashioned. She just looked like herself. Her eyes had the same brown warmth they'd always had.

"What is your Early Present to be, then, Sal?" Gran asked.

"The one from you," Sal said instantly, not knowing why that was the one she wanted most to see.

"Well, it's not anything new or glamorous," Gran said, a bit mischievously.

She handed Sal a small package, wrapped in bright paper. Sal opened it slowly, making it last a long time.

When the wrapping was off at last, Sal stared. There, in her hands, was a carved wooden box. On the top, its wings delicately

shaped in wood and painted a glowing orange and black, was a Monarch butterfly.

"I've been saving it," Gran said. "Your Grandad and I didn't have a daughter, but your Dad and Mother gave us a very fine grand-daughter. I've kept this to give you the year you were ten. My father carved it and my mother painted it, and they gave it to me the year I was ten."

Sal turned the box over in her hands. She read the words on

the underside. *To Sarah, from her loving parents.* Only now did she recall whom she had been named after. The name Sal was short for Sarah.

Sal looked at Gran, and her heart thudded.

"Gran, it's beautiful. I'll always cherish it."

Where did those words come from? Sal knew they didn't

sound exactly like her, and yet she knew she meant them. She'd heard somebody say them, and now she couldn't quite remember who or when. She knew only that this Christmas was one she would remember all her life.

"I know you will," Gran said. "It's what I guess you could call a family heirloom, now. You know, I nearly lost it, the very day I was first given it. Nearly lost it in the snow."

"How did you find it?" Sal asked curiously.

Gran smiled. It was a faraway smile, and yet it was close as well.

"It's the oddest thing," Gran said. "I never could quite remember, afterwards."

*   *   *   *

Special thanks to Dr. H.E. Gastle
of Lakefield, Ontario, whose
woods, sleighs and horses provided
the models for those in this story.
M.L.
M.W.